MW01143631

Soft Stuff

Copyright 1993 • All Rights Reserved

Story of the Toothfairie
1st Edition
1998

Printed in U.S.A
ESP Printing Inc. • Kent, Washington

ISBN 0-9664799-0-4

Dedication

For Rian,
She believes in dreams…
She believes in me.

The Story of the Toothfairie

The Story of the Toothfairie

It's been a long time since the Toothfairie has been happy. We haven't shown how much we love her, and she feels lonely. She has only one job, and it's very important. She's the one who helps you take care of your teeth. She loves them so, and that's why she saves them.

Have you ever wondered where the Toothfairie lives? Well, I can tell you her house has two rooms in it. One she calls the "Great Teeth Room". She keeps the great ones in there. The other she calls the "Not-So-Great Teeth Room". What do you suppose she keeps in there?

The Toothfairie has been pretty disappointed with the teeth she's been picking up lately. It seems that some kids don't like to brush, and they eat more candy. This makes the Toothfairie sad because the "Not-So-Great Teeth Room" has more in it right now.

Whenever she goes to the "Great Teeth Room" her heart starts to sing a little. She has to wear sunglasses because beautiful light from clean, shiny teeth comes out when she opens the door. She breathes deeply because it smells SO good in there! In no time at all her heart is full of happiness!

Everytime I hear a child humming while they brush their teeth I know the Toothfairie just opened her favorite door!

Then she has to check the "Not-So-Great Teeth Room". The Toothfairie takes off her sunglasses, gets her flashlight and nose plugs, and heads for the door. She doesn't like this part of her job, and I'll bet you can guess why!

The Toothfairie gets upset when she hears kids say:

"I don't want to go to the Dentist!"

She can't understand that because she knows that the Dentist helps you keep your teeth clean. YOU DON'T WANT ANY CAVITIES, DO YOU? No cavities means you are doing a great job.

Speaking of jobs, collecting your teeth has it's problems. It's hard for the Toothfairie to get under that great big pillow on your bed! Kids are smarter these days so their heads are heavier! Sometimes the tooth she's after gets lost in all the moving around you do while you sleep. Oh, she gets SO weepy when she loses even one of your precious teeth!

The Toothfairie needed a partner; someone who would stay quiet while you sleep. She decided to take a walk and think. When she stepped outside she saw Mr. Butterfly busy drinking the nectar from the flowers in the garden. The Toothfairie told him about her problems, and asked for his help. Mr. Butterfly was happy to help. He knows how big her job is, and he loves a great smile as much as the Toothfairie does.

Ever since that time, the Toothfairie and Mr. Butterfly have been working together to help kids, like you, take care of their teeth.

I remember a little girl who was so excited because one of her baby teeth was coming loose. Her name was Emma, and she was such a nice little girl. There was only one problem; she didn't take care of her teeth! Sometimes she didn't tell the truth about brushing, and she would even fall asleep with gum in her mouth!

The day Emma's tooth fell out she sat on her bed and looked at it for the longest time. Emma could hardly wait for night to come! She wondered what the Toothfairie would leave for her as she fell happily asleep.

Mr. Butterfly wasn't smiling. He was upset because he knew the Toothfairie was not going to be happy about Emma's tooth. When the Toothfairie came to get Emma's tooth, Mr. Butterfly looked away because he couldn't stand to see her sad, sad face.

Emma suddenly awoke to the most pitiful sound she had ever heard. She sat up in bed and saw the Toothfairie sitting on her pillow, holding her tooth, crying! Emma said; "Oh Toothfairie, why are you crying?"

The Toothfairie replied; "Because I have to put this tooth in the "Not-So-Great Teeth Room", and that makes me so sad!"

Emma's heart broke in two sitting there, on her bed, in the dark. She was very sorry. Mr. Butterfly watched, and wished there was something he could do. He felt so hopeless that his wings began to droop and lose all their beautiful color.

The Toothfairie said; "I don't understand why kids don't like to brush their teeth when it tastes so good. I think a clean, fresh mouth tastes better than any candy."

Emma smiled because the Toothfairie was right! Brushing your teeth DOES taste good! So good that she wanted to jump out of bed, right then, and brush 'em up!

Emma leaned close to the Toothfairie and said; "I'm sorry to make you cry. I promise to brush my teeth two times, every single day, from now on."

The Toothfairie slowly lifted her head until she was looking straight into Emma's eyes…………………and smiled! Emma had to hold her breath because the shiny, bright, beauty of the Toothfairie's smile made her dark room glow! Can you imagine such loveliness?

Well, it was time for the Toothfairie and Mr. Butterfly to leave. Emma could see that he was feeling much better, because his wings weren't drooping at all. Mr. Butterfly looked magnificent with all his colors shining! The Toothfairie turned to wave, and smile, at Emma once more as they left through her bedroom window.

Emma snuggled down again in her warm, soft covers. She decided, as she went back to sleep, to have a smile as beautiful as the Toothfairie's, and a heart just as kind.

Two days later, while Emma was brushing her teeth, she saw a flash of light come from her mouth. She moved closer to the mirror and what do you suppose she saw? A beautiful new tooth growing where the other fell out! Emma was so excited that every time she passed a mirror she would run to look at her new tooth again. Oh, how she wished the Toothfairie knew!

That night Emma sat on her bed and wished with all her might for the Toothfairie and Mr. Butterfly to visit her again to see her new tooth. In the morning, when Emma awoke, there was a tiny flower from the Toothfairie's garden resting on her pillow!

So, the next time you lose one of your precious teeth, relax! Mr. Butterfly will help make sure the Toothfairie gets it.

Brush 'em up! Every single day! If you do, you'll be proud of your teeth, and, the Toothfairie will be proud of YOU!

Oh, I just love the Toothfairie! Don't you?

The End

You Color It!

You Color It!

The Story of The TOOTHFAIRIE ORDER FORM

SOFT STUFF
4742 42nd Ave. SW, Ste 386
Seattle, WA 98116
(206) 650-3392

PURCHASE ORDER

Name: _____

Address: _____

City: _____ State: _____ Zip: _____ Phone: _____

QTY.	DESCRIPTION	BOY	GIRL	PRICE	TOTAL
	The Story of The Toothfairie			$12.99	
				Sub Total	
				Shipping & Handling	$4.49
				Taxes State	
				TOTAL	

METHOD OF PAYMENT:

❏ A check (payable to **SOFT STUFF**) is attached

❏ Charge my ❏ MasterCard ❏ VISA ❏ Amex

Card Number_____ Exp. Date: _____
                                                    MO/YR

_____
Please print name as it appears on card

_____
Signature (required for credit card purchases)

The Story of The TOOTHFAIRIE ORDER FORM

SOFT STUFF
4742 42nd Ave. SW, Ste 386
Seattle, WA 98116
(206) 650-3392

PURCHASE ORDER

Name: _____

Address: _____

City: _____ State: _____ Zip: _____ Phone: _____

QTY.	DESCRIPTION	BOY	GIRL	PRICE	TOTAL
	The Story of The Toothfairie			$12.99	
				Sub Total	
				Shipping & Handling	$4.49
				Taxes State	
				TOTAL	

METHOD OF PAYMENT:

☐ A check (payable to **SOFT STUFF**) is attached

☐ Charge my   ☐ MasterCard   ☐ VISA   ☐ Amex

Card Number_____ Exp. Date: _____
                                                MO/YR

_____
Please print name as it appears on card

_____
Signature (required for credit card purchases)